ALPHONSE AND ARCHIBALD
Written and Illustrated by RUTH M. COLLINS

This amusing story shows how it is possible for different nationalities to live in peace on this continent. Two dogs of opposite breeds and temperaments—an English mastiff and a French poodle—together save the lives of the settlers from an Indian massacre at a time when French and English forces were opposing each other for control. The dogs are completely different, but become good friends. Wonderful pictures.

* *

ALPHONSE AND ARCHIBALD

Books by Ruth M. Collins

SEPTIMUS, THE ST. BERNARD
HORACE, THE HOUND THAT HOWLED
ALPHONSE AND ARCHIBALD

ALPHONSE & ARCHIBALD

By Ruth M. Collins

THIS SPECIAL EDITION IS PUBLISHED BY ARRANGEMENT WITH
THE PUBLISHERS OF THE REGULAR EDITION
DODD, MEAD & CO., INC.
BY
E. M. HALE AND COMPANY
EAU CLAIRE, WISCONSIN

Library of Congress Catalog Card Number: 53-9952
Printed in the United States of America

The characters and situations in this book are wholly fictional
and imaginative: they do not portray and are not intended
to portray any actual persons or parties.

TO MY FRENCH AND ENGLISH FRIENDS

IN THE PROVINCE OF QUEBEC

ALPHONSE AND ARCHIBALD

Alphonse was a French poodle and, like most poodles, very, very clever. He lived, many years ago, with his young master, François Dufour, in a small settlement on the south bank of the St. Lawrence River. The settlement was made up of a dozen long, narrow farms running down to the river's edge and a wooden fort where the *seigneur* (or nobleman) lived with his soldiers.

From time to time the seigneur had to go to France, to pay homage to his overlord, King Louis XIV. As a special mark of favor, His Majesty had given him the poodle. The seigneur (who had expected a gift of money and who did not like dogs, anyway) promptly gave Alphonse to his godson, François Dufour.

Alphonse was a handsome creature. He had twinkling black eyes and a proud way of walking.

When he first appeared at the farmhouse, where François lived with his grandmother, his curly black coat was cut and clipped in the strangest fashion. He even had a large bow of ribbon on top of his head.

Grandmère, seated at her spinning wheel by the fire, threw up her hands when she saw the odd-looking creature.

"A poodle," she cried, "when what we need is a strong dog to help with the farm work!"

"But Grandmère," protested François "the seigneur told me that poodles are the cleverest dogs in the world. You can teach them to do anything. Alphonse, *salute* Grandmère!"

Alphonse promptly sat up and bobbed his head three times.

Grandmère chuckled.

"A true Frenchman," she cried. "His manners are perfect. But here, in New France, manners are not enough. Dogs, as well as men, must work if they wish to live."

François said nothing, for he knew she was right. Besides, nobody contradicted his grandmother.

Grandmère was a power in the little settlement and everyone, from the seigneur down, respected her wise judgment and shrewd tongue. Her husband and her sons had been killed by Indians and since then she and François had managed her tiny farm together.

The days that followed were strange and busy ones for Al-phonse, who had always been a pampered pet. But he was strong and very quick to learn. In no time at all François had him har-nessed to a small cart, hauling loads of firewood. He drove the sheep and cattle to pasture, hunted rabbits with François and learned to fetch and carry for Grandmère.

He was most attentive to the old lady—especially when she was cooking.

Because the poodle had such keen eyes and ears, François taught him to bark a warning whenever strangers came near the settlement, for although there had been no active fighting for some years, the settlers still lived in fear of raids from the Dutch and English colonies to the South and from bands of wandering Iroquois Indians.

By the time his clipped coat had grown long and curly, Alphonse had become a true pioneer dog.

One morning François heard the poodle's warning bark in the field at the back of the house. He snatched up his father's old musket and ran out to find a fair-haired boy crouching against the fence. Beside him was the biggest, saddest dog François had ever seen.

Why, it's as big as a calf, he thought as he ran up.

Alphonse barked shrilly. He thought it *was* a calf. The boy's face was covered with dirt and scratches, and his clothes were in rags. His voice cracked with weariness as he said, "I mean you no harm. I've lost my way."

François scowled furiously. The boy spoke in French but so haltingly that it was clearly not his mother tongue.

"You're English," François cried fiercely and the boy nodded.

"I'm Phineas Ford," he said simply. "I was a passenger on my uncle's ship when it was wrecked in a fog at the mouth of this river. My dog and I managed to swim ashore. We have been wandering for days in these woods. Can you help me? I am trying to find my way south to the English colonies."

François shook his head. Never would he help an English boy.

"You are my prisoner," he said sternly. With his musket held at the boy's back, François marched the stranger up to the fort and turned him over to the captain of the guard. The big dog trailed behind them, taking no notice of Alphonse, who danced in circles around him.

The captain questioned the prisoner closely. He also scowled fiercely when Phineas admitted that he was English.

"Lock him in the guardhouse," he said. "I must speak to the seigneur about this."

He hurried away while the soldiers locked up the prisoner.

The big dog settled himself outside the door of the guardhouse. He was a noble-looking creature, with a black muzzle and great sad eyes. His name was Archibald—and it did not suit him.

Alphonse, who had never seen an English mastiff before, stood watching him with his head cocked on one side. He wished the big dog would play with him. He began to dance up and down in front of the mastiff, barking and wagging his tail. Archibald just stared over his head and looked sadder than ever.

This annoyed Alphonse. He bared his teeth and began to growl. He walked, stiff-legged around Archibald, inviting him to fight.

Archibald gave a huge yawn and shut his eyes.

"Aha!" cried the soldiers who were watching. "He is a coward, the big dog!"

It did not occur to them that Archibald was simply too good-tempered to quarrel—especially with a dog that was so much smaller than himself.

The seigneur summoned all the people to him to decide the fate of the prisoner.

"He is an English spy; shoot him!" shouted the soldiers.

"No, no!" cried the women. "He is only a lad and he is unarmed."

"Fiddlesticks!" snapped Grandmère. "Shooting men when the settlement needs strong, healthy workers! Make him work for his living, aye and his big dog, too."

Grandmère as usual had the last word. Phineas was put to work in the kitchen of the fort. The cook, a fat, short-tempered man, abused him roundly and gave him all the hardest and dirtiest tasks to do. Phineas hated his work but, being English, he just kept a stiff upper lip and got on with his job.

Archibald was given to one of the farmers and as he watched his dog being led away, Phineas said sadly, "Archibald is only a watch dog. You will never make a farm dog of him."

Phineas was right.

One by one, the farmers tried the dog out and, one by one, they gave him up in disgust. Orders (which Alphonse understood and obeyed instantly) meant nothing to Archibald. He only looked bewildered. His deep, roaring bark terrified the animals and scattered them in all directions. He was good-natured and tried to do his best, but he was too big and too clumsy. He knocked over the milk pails and trampled on the eggs. One sweep of his tail would clear the dishes off the table. Finally, when he was harnessed to

a cart, he just sat down and refused to move. As a farm dog Archibald was a complete failure. The farmers jeered at him. Alphonse ignored him completely. He spent his days wandering in the woods, or hanging about the kitchen door, watching his master at work. He was *very* unhappy.

Only Grandmère and the other women were kind to him and fed him. They had discovered that the big dog was very gentle and patient with all young children and small creatures. Often they would coax him into their kitchens to look after the children while they worked in the fields.

One hot day in July a messenger arrived at the fort. He came from the Governor, who lived in Quebec, to summon the seigneur and all his men to an important meeting.

The seigneur called together his soldiers and all his tenant farmers who could bear arms, and sailed up the river to Quebec. Four soldiers, with the help of the old men, were left to guard the fort, while the women and young boys managed the farm work.

Two days later, as Archibald was wandering in the woods overlooking the river, he saw François, with Alphonse at his heels, striding along the path in front of him. He stood and stared after them sadly for he was very lonely and longed to be invited to join them. But they vanished around a bend in the trail without looking back.

Suddenly Archibald heard the poodle barking furiously. Next there came a muffled cry from François and the sound of bodies threshing about in the bushes. For a moment Archibald stood motionless, then he raced forward to see what was the matter.

As he crashed through the bushes he saw François and a strange, painted creature struggling together on the edge of the bank that sloped steeply down to the river. Alphonse, his teeth bared and his hair bristling with rage, was circling about them.

The Indian, with one hand clutching François by the throat, flung up his right arm. The sun flashed on the blade of his tomahawk as Archibald, with a deep coughing roar, launched himself on the man. The full force of his one hundred and eighty pounds struck the Indian squarely on the chest. The savage staggered, overbalanced, and rolled down the steep bank into the river. But as he fell the dog's teeth ripped off a strip of his buckskin shirt.

François stood for a moment, coughing and rubbing his throat. Then he bent and patted the mastiff's head.

"Good dog, Archibald," he croaked.

He turned and raced for home. Alphonse started to follow him —then stopped and looked back at the mastiff. Archibald looked at Alphonse, and suddenly both dogs' tails began to wave in the friendliest way. They touched noses briefly and then, side by side, they galloped after François. But Archibald still held the strip of buckskin in his teeth.

Grandmère's face was grave as she took the strip from the big dog's mouth. She looked carefully at the pattern of beadwork on it.

"Iroquois," she said to François. "If they are in the neighborhood, there is no time to be lost!"

She tied the buckskin around the poodle's neck. "Alphonse, go rouse the people!" she cried.

Then she and François hurried to the fort, with Archibald gamboling about them like a skittish calf. Alphonse no longer ignored him and François had called him a good dog. No wonder Archibald was feeling very pleased with himself.

Alphonse ran from farmhouse to farmhouse, barking loudly. When the settlers saw the buckskin they knew at once that the settlement was in danger.

One and all they came running to the fort.

"Oh, what shall we do, with the seigneur and all our men at Quebec?" wailed the women.

"Fight!" shouted the old men and the soldiers.

Grandmère snorted.

"With what?" she cried. "Half a dozen muskets between the lot of you? No my friends, this must be a battle—not of bullets —but of wits. I have a plan."

Everyone stopped shouting to listen to her.

"The Iroquois," said Grandmère, "like two things—fighting and feasting. Well, we will fight them with food. We will prepare a special feast, one-of-those-at-which-everyone-must-keep-eating-until-the-host-gives-the-sign-to-stop. It is an old Iroquois custom. They will have to eat until they are unable to move. Then we can slip away to the boats. Is my plan good?"

"Yes, yes," cried the settlers. Only Phineas was silent.

When just a child he had been captured by the Iroquois. They had adopted him into the tribe and taught him their language. When he escaped some years later, he knew all about their craft and their cruelty.

Grandmère set everyone to work. The boys were sent to the river to spread the nets for eels and fish. The children rounded

up the chickens and collected the eggs. The old men drove the sheep, cows and pigs into the fort, while François, Alphonse and the soldiers scattered through the woods to watch for the Iroquois. Grandmère, Phineas and all the women stoked the fires and prepared the great feast. Archibald watched them with his tongue hanging out.

Soon the most tantalizing smells rose into the air.

It was almost sunset when François, Alphonse and the soldiers came racing back to the fort.

"They are coming!" they gasped. "Hundreds of them! We saw them crossing the stream down in the valley."

"Throw open the gates," cried Grandmère. "Muzzle the dogs and tie them up. Soldiers, hide yourselves in the guardhouse but keep your muskets ready in case there is trouble."

This was done and everyone waited, tingling with excitement and fear. For half an hour quiet reigned. Then all at once the woods rang with the dreaded war cry and the Iroquois, in gleaming war paint, came racing through the trees toward the fort.

U. S. 1162104

In front of the open gates they stopped abruptly, puzzled and uncertain what to do. Instead of the bullets they had expected, they were met by the fragrant smells of roasting pigs and frying chicken. For some time they held back, suspecting a trap, but finally the mouth-watering smells overcame their caution. With their chief at their head, they filed slowly into the fort.

In front of them were long trestle-tables, covered with bowls and platters of steaming food. Grandmère stood at the head table. Behind her were François, Phineas and a group of pale-faced women.

The chief advanced toward Grandmère. There was a savage gleam in his eyes as he raised his tomahawk. Grandmère's face went as white as her kerchief, but she did not move a muscle.

Suddenly Phineas stepped forward. He lifted his arm in the Indian style of greeting. In the Iroquois tongue he addressed the chief, explaining the nature of the feast and bidding him welcome.

Slowly the chief's arm sank to his side. The cruel glitter faded from his eyes, and when Phineas paused for breath, he thanked the boy in a speech that lasted ten minutes.

"Ah, the brave Phineas!" muttered Grandmère as, with trembling limbs, she seated herself at the head table. François and Phineas threw more logs on the fires, the Indians crowded around the food—and the feast was on.

All through the night the Indians feasted. More and more food was brought out and set before them. When the day dawned most of them were feeling distinctly uncomfortable. Their heads sagged over the tables and their eyes were almost closed. But Grandmère still sat in her place, and until she stood up nobody could stop eating. As the Indians grew sleepier and sleepier the women and children slipped away, one by one. They were followed by the old men and boys and finally by the soldiers—until only Grandmère, François and Phineas were left.

When Grandmère saw that the chief himself had fallen under the table, she stood up. Her guests gave a sigh of relief, staggered to their feet—and promptly fell flat on their faces.

François and Phineas released the dogs and, with Grandmère, hurried down to the river. The others had taken the boats. Only a birchbark canoe was left.

Alphonse leaped nimbly into the canoe and settled himself in the bow, but Archibald whimpered and backed away from the frail-looking craft.

Grandmère tore her apron into strips.

"Tie up his legs," she ordered.

Archibald was trussed up like a chicken and bundled into the canoe. Grandmère took his head in her lap, the boys seized the paddles and they started on their long journey up the river.

The sun was setting by the time they reached the next settlement. Here they found the rest of their party, who were being cared
for by friendly settlers. Grandmère was welcomed with open arms.
She was taken to a farmhouse and put to bed.

François and Phineas fell asleep in front of the kitchen fire
while Alphonse and Archibald snored at their feet.

Next day François and the soldiers sailed on to Quebec to carry the news of the raid to the seigneur. Alphonse accompanied his master, but Archibald was left with Phineas to watch over Grandmère. The settlers no longer looked upon Phineas as an enemy and a spy. His prompt action had saved all their lives and earned him their lasting gratitude.

Grandmère was loud in her praises and treated him as though he were her own son.

At the end of the week François and Alphonse returned with the seigneur. As well as his own men, the seigneur brought with him a company of soldiers, assigned to him by the Governor. With the women and children they all sailed back to their settlement.

The fort was deserted when they arrived, for the Iroquois, on recovering their wits, had slipped silently away. But the seigneur was not certain that they would not return. The soldiers were posted as guards around the settlement while the men set about reinforcing the defences of the fort.

That evening the seigneur ordered a big fire to be lighted and called all the people together to discuss plans for the future. As he rose to speak to them, his eye fell on Phineas. He called the boy to him.

"Phineas," he said, "you were a prisoner and our enemy. Yet, by your quickness and wit, you saved the lives of our women and children. You have earned our respect and gratitude. I now set you free. I will give you provisions and men to guide you on your journey south."

Phineas blushed and looked very uncomfortable. To his amazement, he found he had no desire to leave these hot-tempered, warm-hearted people.

Grandmère spoke up.

"Fie, fie, Seigneur," she said. "Do not send away a good lad when this settlement needs men. Besides, I like the boy. My home shall be his home, if he wishes to stay with us."

Then she laughed and pointed to Archibald, who was stretched out full-length in front of the fire. Alphonse was curled up against him, with his nose resting on the big dog's shoulder.

"See," she said, "the dogs have set the example. Let their masters follow it."

She turned and looked at her grandson. François hesitated not a moment. He held out his hand to the English boy. With a friendly smile, Phineas stepped forward and grasped it firmly.

The seigneur clapped his approval while the men set up a cheer.

In front of the fire the two dogs opened their eyes—sighed in utter contentment—and went to sleep again, close together.